Some Thoughts in Rhyme

by Steve Rosen

RoseDog Books
PITTSBURGH, PENNSYLVANIA 15238

RoseDog Books
585 Alpha Drive
Suite 103
Pittsburgh, PA 15238
Visit our website at *www.rosedogbookstore.com*

ISBN: 979-8-88812-250-1
eISBN: 979-8-88812-750-6

Some Thoughts in Rhyme

Some of these poems will make you laugh.

Some may make you want to cry.

But hopefully, all of them will have you thinking.

Dedication

This collection is dedicated to my wife Marilyn, whom I have loved since the first time I saw her more than fifty-five years ago walking down that college hallway when we were both just twenty.

Table of Contents

Poetry Reading Night 1
Some Old Guy Thoughts 2
A Grandfather's Wish 4
Special Visits 5
Our Grandkids Say the Darnedest Things 7
Hair? 9
My Body 11
Old Folks Should Never Step Backwards 14
We Can't Sleep 17
My Root Canal 20
The Cold 22
Planning New Year's Eve 24
The Florida Question 26
The Heat 28
Book Club 30
The Deer Question 33
How About a Sweater? 35
Oh Great, a Wedding Invite! 37
Thoughts For the Young Married 39
Together Forever 40
A Flight to Paradise 43
Why a Child? 46
I Wake, Do Nothing, Sleep 48
Bad Luck? 50
Decisions 52
The Room 54
A Hundred Billion Stars in the Galaxy 56
A Sad Reality 58
The Hill 59
Here We All Lie, We Died 60
Just Another Life 61
Sin, Prayer, G-d's Mercy 62
Fall at the Beach 65

Poetry Reading Night

I attended my first ever poetry reading night
And yes, I did read a poem there, that's right

The event was headlined by two guest presenters
Followed by some eighteen of us hopeful pretenders

My wife came to provide me with moral support
And perhaps to ensure I wouldn't just simply abort

It's true I didn't have a clue as to what to expect
And by this writing I mean no poet any disrespect

There must have been some thirty poems read in all
And truly as best as I can honestly recall

My reading was the one and only time
That the verses of a poem actually rhymed!

Emily and Walt paved the way for free verse poetry
A novel concept allowing poetic form to be free

But I wonder, oh how I wonder, if they were here today,
What they would think of "poetry" that doesn't rhyme in any way

Rhyming words with purpose seems a more difficult job to do
Maybe that's why "poets" have given rhyme in poems ado

Emily and Walt will always have my highest regard
But if your writings do not rhyme, are you really a bard?

Some Old Guy Thoughts

I still have all my fingers and toes
I still remember how most things go
My back and knees are a little weak
And I confess some trouble taking a leak

I'm retired for more than fifteen years
My opinions fall on mostly deaf ears
No one cares what I have to say
Not like it was back in the day

My experience doesn't count anymore
My thoughts are just ancient folklore
Reminded to always watch what I say
And whatever I do stay out of the fray

A wife to guide me in whatever I do
And kids who think I need their help too
Grandkids too old now to sit on my lap
All quite happy when I retire for a nap

But the old guy still has a moment or two
When the family doesn't know quite what to do
"Old guy" please tell us what do you think
We need your advice to get back from the brink

Well, I say, have you thought about this
And let's be sure that there is nothing we miss
Talking it through, we'll reach a fine end
I'm sure we'll put the problem on the mend

And so the discussion goes on for a while
Sometimes it even ends with a smile
This problem solved this particular day
Goodbye, not thank you, is all that they say

Leave them feeling that they solved it alone
And that you were just a voice on the phone
And on their next visit things revert to the old
"Get Dad a blanket; he looks rather cold."

A Grandfather's Wish

The first time I saw her so tiny and pink
Calm one moment; the next raising a stink
I held her gently, my precious dove
That moment forever winning Pop-Pop's love

Quickly she grew to the girl she is now
Just six and a half and wearing my crown
She reads, writes, draws, plays, and sings
A whirlwind, busy with all sorts of things

Eager to learn and quick as a wit
Dancing and playing and physically fit
Making time for her sister and lovingly so
Wherever she's at that sister's in tow

Barbies, games, parties, and playdates
T-ball and soccer and all of her playmates
Visits to Grandma and to Pop-Pop too
Shopping with Mom; trips with Dad to the zoo

She's half to a teen and half again to full grown
This time is so precious; we have her on loan
Each day that she grows, her horizons expand
Her attention gets taken up by new demands

But though she will venture far from the nest
Hopefully, she'll come home now and then for a rest
With fond memories of her youth filled with delight
And warm thoughts of family if we've done it right

Special Visits

My grandson holds a special place in my heart
I love his visits but hate when he departs
Such energy, he jumps up and hugs me tight
That's a special feeling of pure delight

Then off with his coat and off with his shoes
And of course, time for mine to come off too
Pick a book or two from the shelf to read
We race to the couch, he's in the lead

Sometimes we go out for lunch
His favorite place, the diner, I have a hunch
Chicken fingers, I'm pretty sure
The ones shaped like tiny dinosaurs

After lunch we take a walk around the block
Always active, he'll throw a stick; kick a rock
His visits keep me young and are the best
But when he leaves I welcome a rest!

Our Grandkids Say the Darnedest Things

Our grandkids say the darnedest things
So much joy their sayings can bring
The four of ours have gifted us with a few
So here are some without further ado

Our oldest at the time was just about four
Standing by our family room door
Clearly, she had something to say
Which she did exactly this way

You see, we had a beautiful dollhouse
She would sit and play with it quiet as a mouse
Visit after visit until she had the courage to say
"What for Grandma needs a dollhouse anyway?"

Our only grandson, was five at the time
Lived in Manhattan, which he liked just fine
He visited us at our home in suburban N.J.
And I guess the difference just blew him away

Grandma took him for a walk around the block
It seems the experience was a culture shock
Because halfway around he blurted this out
"Grandma, why are there no people about?"

Now our second granddaughter is a lively one
Never by her older sister to be outdone
Always watching to be sure to get her share
To be sure we try to treat them all fair

The older one was leaving for college the next day
So we gave her spending money to ease her way
The younger one stood next to her toe to toe
And said "Grandma, I have expenses too, you know."

The best was said by our youngest one
She thought having a dog would be fun
We helped get her family a havapoo
They named her Lexi; her brother was happy too

Well you know how puppies can be
And Lexi at times would bark incessantly
Her patience lost and sometimes not easily found
Said "Gather your things Lexi, you're off to the pound."

Let me leave you with this important thought
By even the youngest among us we can be taught
And often the very unfiltered things they say
Are the best things we're blessed to come our way

Hair?

From the time I can remember,
my father had very little hair.
And as I can best recall,
he really didn't seem to care.

To be sure, it's true,
he had some on the sides.
And everyone would tell me,
it's a sign that he was wise.

As a boy growing up,
my hair was quite the mop.
It grew so thick and quickly,
it just wouldn't stop.

All through my twenties,
it stayed quite the same.
And into my thirties,
I still had quite a nice mane.

In my forties I could see,
just the bit of a change.
But in my humble opinion,
it did not look at all strange.

Well, folks, the fifties,
brought some changes for sure.
Graying and thinning hair,
and it was not premature.

In my sixties I retired
and I was free to do this.
A smooth shaved head,
those last few hairs I don't miss.

My Body

I always hoped you'd be my friend
Till my life's very, very end
In retrospect, it was a lot to ask
Quite the unrealistic task

I still remember when we were young
We'd romp and play; fearless fun
Ten stitches that time on my face
Sliding headlong into third base

Baseball was our first test of skill
Off stoops and wall; endless drills
Little League, the first formal test
You helped make me one of the best

I was always small for my age
At each and every growing-up stage
All the more reason to rely on you
To help me play the sports I do

The older I got the more serious the play
But you stuck with me every day
Playing as much as I did
From the time I was just a little kid

Basketball was the last to go
Lost my bounce and a step too slow
Knees hurting from the very first step
Getting old, that's what you get

So finally, we put sports aside
Replaced with exercises we tried
I no longer tax you quite so much
But we haven't totally lost our touch

My grandson and I still play catch
And there's the occasional tennis match
True, I might need two days to recover
From all the aches my play uncovered

Maybe if I could relive my youth
I'd better honor this one for-sure truth
Just the one body to last all life long
So treat it with care to keep it strong

People now say I look like my dad
Well, maybe, my face just a tad
But the way I most certainly do
Is from my neck down to my shoes

Lost my firm chest over the years
And this belly; can't blame it on beers
Somehow lost three inches in height
While my weight has gone out of sight

I exercise every day, I really do
To strengthen my back and my knees too
Maybe it's time to find a new way
To help hold off my body's decay

But let's face it; nature has won
My body is reaching the end of its run
But I'm not ready to give up the fight
Where's the heating pad? I'll need it tonight

Old Folks Should Never Step Backwards

As it happened I learned that lesson the hard way
Had an accident on an otherwise uneventful day
Fell backwards in my kitchen making a cup of joe
Landed hard; broke my hip; wouldn't you know

Called out in pain to my wife who came to my aid
"What's wrong; oh my G-d; look at the mess you made"
I fell; I'm in pain; can't get up off the floor
In fact, any attempt to move hurts all the more

She called EMS; their arrival a blessing
A quick assessment; to the hospital I'm going
COVID soaring; protocols in place
The closest hospital the choice in every case

An X-ray confirmed a broken hip
An all-too likely result from a fall or a slip
Surgery set; no choice of your surgeon
With COVID, you're told this will be your person

Waited three days till the surgery could be set
The pain proved stronger than the meds I could get
Post-surgery just one more day they let me stay
Then home to start rehab the very next day

After two weeks I started out-patient therapy
Building strength and balance was the strategy
Taking rehab seriously I gave it a wholehearted try
Adding exercises and reps as the weeks went by

But month after month my hip was not healing
Let's give it more time was my surgeon's feeling
But maybe it was time to seek a second opinion
Clearly I was headed to a second-surgery decision

The first surgery was like an erector set
Screws, pins and a rod where the hip and leg met
Now I'm told any time the screw could come loose
In that event I'd really be a cooked goose

So a second surgery I agreed to have done
And you're right hard choices are no fun
But this time I picked the doc and the place
I just hope my faith was not misplaced

I'm under strict orders as I again try to heal
No weight on the leg for eight weeks is the deal
My wife is helping to insure this time's the charm
And so far no problems, no need for alarm

I'm now looking forward to enjoy better days
Freedom to do more, to come and go as I may
With a new sensitivity toward the handicapped
And an understanding hand that I previously lacked

UP AGAIN
AT 2!
WHY US!

We Can't Sleep

Not being able to sleep is a terrible pain
With us old folks it's a common refrain
Night after night, all night, we just lay in bed
Never finding a comfortable place for our head

We may doze for fifteen minutes or so
And then just wake up for no reason you know
This pattern repeats itself all night long
Night after night it's the very same song

Each night we fall into bed exhausted
But once there we've soon lost it
The fear of not being able to fall asleep
Is the only thought your head will keep

All that leads to a vicious merry-go-round
The fear, no sleep, so little peace I've found
A pill now and then gives some relief
But too much of that is bad, my belief

Sure there are over-the-counter aids
Truth told, I've gotten little for what I've paid
Sure they claim they work much of the time
But you might argue so would a glass of wine

I can go all day long without an itch
Hit that pillow and I start to twitch
If it's my leg; it just needs a scratch or two
But my back requires a lot more effort to do

How often do I leave the bed you ask
Well, that depends on the needed task
A bathroom trip is the number one run
And usually of those there is at least one

Read a book or maybe watch TV
Not much on the tube early morning at three
The daily TV news really starts at four
I'd rather be sleeping; the news is a bore

Since I'm still awake at six, I start my day
Eat right and keep busy helps, they say
And be sure you do some daily exercise
It's really necessary, you'd be surprised

But all day long your head's in a fog
You're just dragging in a terrible slog
And you can't wait to get back into bed
But bed is a place that conjures up dread

So much literature, tips to fall asleep
Not much I've found that I want to keep
Warm or cold room or a setting in-between
Get that right and you'll soon start to dream

Dark room or just a slight touch of light
Again, experts don't agree on what is right
Some quiet music or no noise at all
There seems to be no one expert to call

I know we're not alone my wife and I
Sorry, but that thought hardly mollifies
Tonight I'll give it another try until two
If I'm still up, I'll dream up something to do

My Root Canal

Had my first ever root canal today
Not a choice way to wile your time away
The doc and her assistant on either side
I'm reclined and told to just open wide

"First, we're just going to make you a little numb."
Two shots to my roof and three to my gums
"Now that didn't hurt too, too bad," she said
That's when I realized I should have stayed in bed

A small reprieve to give the meds time to take hold
The worse yet to come, but, of course, I wasn't told
Sooner than I hoped, they began again in earnest
It was time to man up and rise to the coming test

My appointment was scheduled for two long hours
Staying there that long took all my will powers
Remember, I told you the worst was yet to come
It was then the doc got down to the real dental "fun"

She inserted this contraption between my lips
And another block like thing so my bite wouldn't slip
Told to stay like that, mouth open wide, the entire session
What sins had I committed to warrant this torture lesson

All preparations done the drilling now commenced
It was the main event, and it was truly intense
The meds were effective in reducing the pain
But what effect was that pounding having on my brain?

It seemed to take forever to drill and fill that space
I'm thinking be careful, but could you pick up the pace
My back is starting to hurt, and I have to pee
And I can't wait another minute to be set free

Finally, finally doc said we're all done
Well, just a few more x-rays before I let you run
And take these pain meds for the next two days
And rinse your mouth to keep bacteria away

Your tooth will be sore for another week to ten days
So here's some advice you really need to obey
Try chewing only on the other side
It's really the very best solution we've seen tried

And call your dentist so they can follow up
Fill it or cap it; it still needs to be closed up
I then realized that trip we were planning to take
Due to the cost of all this we'd have to forsake

My son said, "Dad you know it's your own damn fault."
And for that, he's right; I really have no retort
So I promise to try to forgo those sweet treats
And as for brushing and flossing, I'll try not to cheat

The Cold

Year after year we suffer the cold
Every year seems worse as we grow old
From November right through May
It's dark, cold, and always so gray

And while I'll grant you NJ's not Chicago
The cold wind here can certainly blow
And we get our share of piling snow
Sometimes as late as April you know

The temperature can fall to zero or less
Snow-clogged streets make driving a mess
The loss of power a very real fear
No choice I'm told but to persevere

If it sounds like I'm complaining
I'm not; I'm just, well, explaining
As I sit here writing these thoughts
I'm personally more and more distraught

You see it's only the start of December
And as noted above you'll remember
I still have five months of this till May
That's every day both night and day

And since I've brought up the night
It's winter; there's far too little light
It's dark each day as early as four
We're shut in our houses behind closed doors

So much cream I have to apply to my skin
It's a game I can't seem to ever win
Dry and cracked and so painful it gets
Haven't found a solution to my dry skin yet

And the first greeting from friends you meet
Is weather related and a wish for some heat
Some have plans for a trip to some place warm
By the thousands to Florida they swarm

And we also have places we'd like to go
Places to escape the cold and the snow
But that escape is only for a month or so
Then back to where those cold winds blow

For better or worse, the cold is part of my life
It's a compromise between me and my wife
For her I'll bear the cold each year
And she'll ignore my winter-long sneer

Planning New Year's Eve

My wife and her friends are planning for New Year's Eve
Simple? No, the complexities are difficult to conceive
One group decided to go local for dinner and dance
Make a decision or soon you'll lose out on the chance

So, the ones who hadn't made up their minds
Huddled together under the pressure of time
And by huddled I mean the texts/emails started to fly
To reach agreement or consensus, the six would try

Twenty texts later they agreed on what would be fine
Just dinner, back to someone's home, cake and wine
The next twenty texts to decide who would host
My wife and I volunteered; we'd give up the ghost

Two of the group had previously hosted events
Excusing them was without dissent or argument
The remaining three would have the honor next year
They can decide together who next would volunteer

That settled, there was still work to be done
They focused their talents to tackle the next big one
Upon which restaurant should they bestow their grace
Can you imagine six ladies trying to agree on a place

Well, it should be someplace not far, reasonably near
Concern for drunk drivers and freezing roads they feared
And a BYO is usually the preferred restaurant choice
And one where it's possible to talk over the noise

So the restaurant choices were narrowed to a few
And one was finally chosen after a bit of a to-do
Complicated by what time the reservation should be for
Eight, maybe seven thirty, but certainly nothing before

So the texts flew around and around once more
Is it me or is this event becoming a bit of a chore
Thank G-d the men were spared from the planning
Although, secretly flames they might have been fanning

I'll spare you the fuss over the cakes and the wines
Who would bring what in the end came out fine
But not before a ton more emails and texts flew
Finally the texts, emails, and planning were through

I, for one, marvel seeing these woman in action
Once they have a purpose, they're quick to gain traction
Along the way there may be small quarrels and fights
But time after time in the end things come out right

New Year's Eve as of this writing is some weeks away
But I'm actually looking forward to hosting that day
With my wife of whom I'm so very, very proud
And celebrating New Year's with this warm, friendly crowd

The Florida Question

Should we winter in New Jersey or to Florida should we go?
That's the question; the answer I just don't know
Let's give it some thought and lay out all the pros and cons
And maybe using that approach, the answer we'll come upon

We've gone to Florida every winter for twenty-plus years
We're getting older and New Jersey's too cold to stay here
True, planning, packing, traveling, and getting settled there
Can be and often has been quite the arduous bear

And it's true the weather in Florida can vary greatly
Particularly the winter months starting in January
And there can be long periods of heavy rain and storms
But the one virtue it has over New Jersey is that it's warm

Every year we've worried about the place we'd be staying
Our history with seasonal rentals most times was dismaying
And more than a few times we packed up and left early
Another day in that place not happening clearly

Now Delray Beach is the town where we most like to stay
It's got nice hotels, restaurants, golf and bridge convenient to play
And of course the ocean walk and the beach are just steps away
All the activities we enjoy more than fill out our day

And over the years we've made so many nice friends
We look forward to seeing them this year once again
And yes, we have family in South Florida as well
They'd be quite disappointed if we didn't come for a spell

So with all of those pros what is it that is keeping us back
It's the end of November and we need to be starting to pack
It's that thing that has hindered many of us again this year
The Corona virus persists and simply refuses to disappear

Now one could argue the virus is the virus here or there
And it's also true that the virus persists here like everywhere
But in New Jersey we have the comforts of our home
And we view our home as affording us a protective dome

We don't need to travel through airports or get on a plane
The thought of a plane ride even in good times is such a pain
Staying in a hotel we'd need to take our meals dining out
That and in-season crowds is what hotel living would be about

And if you believe the stories about Florida that you hear
Folks there don't socially distance or even masks wear
A long stay in Florida, how safe from the virus would you be?
Certainly the risk of infection has to rise exponentially

So despite all the reasons that prompt us to want to go
Fear of the virus has cautioned us to proceed slow
Our best course may be to delay a decision, wait and see
With the current variants even a vaccine isn't a guarantee

But ugh, every day it grows more cold and dark
Soon it will be too cold to take a walk in the park
That hotel reservation we made all those months ago
Wouldn't it be an awful shame for us to just let it go

The Heat

Previously, I wrote a poem about the cold
My dislike of the cold that poem certainly told
But extreme heat solicits a similar emotion
Fear! The real fear of a power disruption

As day after day the heat soars to ninety-five
Can Public Service keep the power grid alive?
And as those temperatures rise day after day
My nerves can't help but begin to fray

Once out, how long will a power failure last
Of course there's hope it will come back fast
But as the hours crawl by, our hopes shrink
And by night that first day, they totally sink

That's when worry becomes all-consuming
The feeling of hopelessness has us fuming
Our neighbors, of course, are all similarly stuck
It seems we're all hit with the same bad luck

No power, no AC, seek any cool place to be
It can be life or death particularly for the elderly
To a mall, a movie, any cool place to flee
And try sleeping; forget it; it's a misery

How long before all the food starts to spoil
Darkness, candles, flashlights, lamps with oil
Just when things seems to be at their worst
A thunder storm hits; you're now really cursed

The torrential rain has found a leak in your roof
You realize your house is not disaster proof
The sump pump has failed since the power is out
The basement now has rising water swishing about

Your family looks to you to save the day
But to you they're more just in the way
You have no magic to bring this disaster to an end
So it's best just to send them to stay with friends

Now alone in the dark, in the sweltering heat
Nature again has dealt you a humbling defeat
Thoughts return to those cold January days
With hope this house will see them again, I pray

So what's worse, a power loss in winter or summer?
Either it seems can be a world-class bummer
Drifting snow or oppressive heat and torrential rain
Frozen pipes or a flooded basement drain

The real question is why are we still in this house
I fear the answer rests solely with my spouse
This house is the only place she wishes to be
And that alone is enough of a reason for me

Book Club

My wife is hosting her book club tonight
For me, that event is not a delight
My choices are either to vacate the house
Or stay upstairs quiet as a mouse

She has the prep pretty much down pat
Some fruit, cake, nuts; stuff like that
The dining room table is the place to eat
And she adorns it with the above chosen treats

The actual discussion takes place in our den
Luckily, we have enough seating for all ten
The ladies come; it's really a social affair
Did everyone read the book? "Yes!" they all swear

For each month's book of choice
One lady has the leadership voice
For a book that she recommended
And approved by all at the last meeting attended

Books chosen can be fiction or nonfiction too
Books allowing for differing points of view
The discussion usually goes about two hours
On display is a wealth of brainpower

Before retiring to the table for treats
The next book is chosen; making the meeting complete
The hostess is responsible to lead that part
Usually, her book recommendation is taken to heart

All in all book club is a fine get-together
Members attend no matter the weather
The only suggestion I might dare to make
Is serve a little wine before, during, and after that cake!

SCAT!

The Deer Question

We live in a nice house in a nice development
Been here forty-six years; that's a real testament
Raised our kids here; grandkids now too play here
It has served us well, that's certainly clear

Our development sits in a small suburban town
As are most of the other towns right around
And none of them have changed much in fifty years
Which brings us the perplexing question of the deer

Over time all these towns have grown more urbanized
Congestion adds to the puzzle, not to criticize
Back when we first moved here all those years ago
There were squirrels, chipmunks, and birds you know

Back then I can't recall seeing even a single deer
Over time now and then a deer or two would appear
And their appearance was truly a welcome sight
If you approached one they would quickly alight

In recent years you'd see a doe and her fawns
Grazing our greens and sleeping on our lawn
They're a sight as they jump from yard to yard
But coaxing them along has become a bit hard

Like our neighbors, we take care of our shrubs
I guess those well-tended shrubs make great grub
And except for watching out for a car here and there
The deer have learned they have little to fear

Recently, there was a herd of deer by my door
A buck, two does, nine fawns and more
They no longer come just at dusk and dawn
All day, if not grazing, they're resting on our lawn!

Our town says; "Sorry there is nothing we can do"
You can't shoot them or trap them; just yell shoo
They stand their ground and defiantly look at you
And don't care if you yell until your face turns blue

A small park sits behind my neighbor's place
That park is the deer's quiet and safe sleeping space
The park is where they run to when scared day or night
But they're back at my place each morning's first light

So why am I troubled by the growing number of deer?
Deer carry tics and the tics carry Lyme disease I fear
And they don't carry their own pooper scooper
Two very good reasons for being a deer party pooper

So I'll continue to yell, bang pots and stamp my feet
And claim a small victory if the herd scampers a retreat
But my success is at best a short-lived victory
I've learned that deer don't have much of a memory

How About a Sweater?

Dick and Jane have been dating for two years
They are fond of each other; that's abundantly clear
Day after day they have treated each other well
Every day their fondness grows; it's easy to tell

So how should they celebrate the two-year date
In a year where COVID most clearly dominates
A nice dinner may be all that's feasible to do
At least until we've seen this pandemic through

To make it special, they agreed to exchange gifts
That decision could very well end up causing a rift
Made even more likely by Dick's firm insistence
"I need nothing"; words he stuck to with persistence

Finally he caved and agreed to a winter sweater
Jane knew she would have to do much better
She knew Dick would give her something nice
Maybe giving five sweaters wouldn't even suffice

Dick, of course, knew what he planned to buy
Jewelry is an easy gift in the mind of every guy
A nice piece of jewelry seemed the best thing
And right to his door the store agreed it to bring

Now Jane's task was tougher if you could believe
She had no magic answer tucked up her sleeve
To the internet she realized she needed to go
Viewing sweaters displayed on pages row after row

Some she bought and had delivered home for review
Most were returned, but she held on to a few
Before she knew it she had collected quite a set
But she wasn't sure there weren't more yet to get

Clearly not asked, nonetheless, her mom piped in
Suggesting more stores prompting new searches to begin
And as the time for gift exchanging grew near
Every day witnessed her growing anxiety and fear

In the end things for both Dick and Jane worked out
Her bracelet was beautiful; her delight never in doubt
And he loved all six sweaters she gifted to him
Leaving the return of the other thirteen soon to begin

The lesson if there is one to be learned from this tale
There may be high stress whether you succeed or fail
But the effort is clearly worth it for the right mate
And seeing them happy left us all feeling great

Oh Great, a Wedding Invite!

I'm happy for Dick and I'm happy for Jane
Forever more they'll share the same last name
The vows were thoughtful; the service was nice
But I'm a bit sorry folks no longer throw rice

We went to their party on that same day
How nice for you most people would say
But the music was loud; the food was bad
And folks only talked about "things" they had

The young folks thought the DJ was hot
The old folks seeking any quiet spot
My wife shouted over and over "never again"
I politely reminded her that this was her friend

Sure there were lots of people we knew
And several we liked, and that's also true
So how many grandkids; how old are they?
Don't see them much; oh, they live far away

Don't get me started on the medical stuff
Stories from strangers that times are tough
Knee and hip replacements galore,
Endless ailments and pains such a bore

And did I mention that the music was loud
Ear plugs hardly muffled the sound
Trying to talk over the music and ear plugs,
Has hurt my throat and maybe damaged my lungs

Now I admit; it's true; I'm getting old
These halls are drafty and I'm frequently cold
Twelve at a table; my friend Bill's across the way
But John is next to me with nothing to say

One bartender for some two hundred guests
Reaching the bar is a herculean test
I returned to the table with two fought-for wines
"I'd rather have a soda, but, dear, take your time"

The father-of-the-bride gave a heartfelt toast
Of course, he thanked his family the most
It's a stretch to say he gave it with poise
Best part—his talk gave relief from the noise

Now I'm not one to ever complain
But that was one small glass of champagne.
The coffee was cold; the desserts were a fight
And for tea you could wait there all night

All these events seemingly follow a trend
But I wish some parts of it I could amend
For example, please cut the cake an hour before
So taking that cue, we can sneak out the door

When it's your party you have a far different view
Well then, the foot's clearly on the other shoe
Keep that in mind when the party's your friends'
Put on a smile and stay until the bitter end

Thoughts For the Young Married

Dick and Jane together are building a life
Not uncommon, it has its stresses and strife
With so much love too, that's plain to see
Together they belong and should forever be

Saving for tomorrow yet needing things now
She's home and at work; she does both somehow
The house needs attention; his job takes its toll
Two steps forward, one back, toward life's goals

But please don't look too far ahead
You've come so far since you were wed
Success is to be measured a day at a time
Focus on that and you'll keep doing fine

A full life together is life's own reward
If it were simpler you'd probably be bored
Overwhelming though today's challenges seem
Tomorrow's, maybe different, will be no less extreme

Your young child today will be a teen tomorrow
You have parents today; their passing a sorrow
Expenses will grow until the kids find their way
Your grandkids will visit to brighten your day

So enjoy today while you plan and dream
Do it together; you make such a great team
You've found each other; there's no better start
Sharing life together; that's the best part

Together Forever

She walked down the hall; his heart skipped a beat
That first moment he knew that they had to meet

They dated and married; two kids right away
Time passed quickly, life's struggles each day

Busy with family; careers on the rise
She managed it all to no one's surprise

The days turned to years; the years to life stages
Kids grown but not gone; keep turning the pages

Now busy with grandkids, she does it all still
Yet eager to explore what lies over the hill

Early life phases, they run their own course
They pull and push you having their own force

Now there's time to ponder; still work or retire?
Difficult choices; what does she desire?

Deciding is stressful; decisions are hard
Discussions seem endless, each on their guard

They'll solve it together; what they're moving toward
Is together, forever; that's their life's reward

CAN THIS GET ANY WORSE?

A Flight to Paradise

Well, I'm finally settled in my middle seat
Vacation just started and I'm already beat
My wife sits by the window at my side
Somehow content to be off on this ride

She's checked three bags for one week away
Almost a bag for each vacation day
In addition, another two under her seat
One of hers under mine; no room for my feet

Any moment now the aisle seat will be taken
More and more I'm dreading this vacation
And as I watch people come down the aisle
I pray for one with a reasonable profile

But true to form my aisle occupant
Looked nothing like someone heaven sent
And right behind me a couple took their seats
With a newborn; how so very, very sweet

Did I mention we were delayed an hour to board
I've noticed they haven't yet closed the door
An announcement; yes, a further delay
"But don't worry we'll soon be on our way"

Two hours later the door's finally closed
Better late than never I suppose
But now I really, really need to take a leak
But the seat sign demands I stay in my seat

Now we're in the air; finally free to alight
But as I arise there's a most dreaded sight
The snack cart has already blocked my path
And there's no release for my pent up wrath

The cart finally passes; to the front it seems clear
But I'm firmly told only first class permitted here
As I retreat to follow the cart down the aisle
A line has formed; it's going to be awhile

In the row ahead a lady reclines her chair
A foot in front of me now rests her hair
As she moves "things" fall on my tray
Did I mention I've been dreading this day

Three hours later we start our descent
Touching ground will be heaven sent
On cue the baby starts his half-hour howl
When I turn to look his dad gives me a scowl

On the ground we have to wait for a gate
That happens when your plane comes in late
Things are grabbed from the overhead bin
You guessed it; I got clipped square on the chin

The board says luggage at carrousel seven
Waiting at seven we're told it's really at eleven
Eight pieces of luggage finally in hand
We're waiting in a long line at the taxi stand

A short week from now we'll do this in reverse
Is it no wonder I find air travel a curse?
Can anyone blame me for dreading this day?
And for never again alighting another jetway

Why a Child?

Baseball cap more off than on
A cyclone through the day
Romping, laughing, doing boy stuff
A handful Grandma would say

Fragile he grew; he slipped away
Taken from our hands
The battle fought; we let him go
Powerless to demand

Not love, nor prayer, nor deed, or anything
Could change that destiny or design
Neither his goodness nor his zest for life
Could mitigate his time

Why him? we ask, we cry, we scream
This child of five, this precious thing
Why now? so young, so promise-filled
Such love to give and joy to bring

Explanations, some would say
Are just not ours to give
Faith in G-d, in a master plan
Is the path down which to live

Others angered, outraged
Take a harder view
No real G-d would allow such a loss
But comforts, they offer few

With G-d's help or not, we can do more
To see us to a brighter day
We can give more than we've given before
And help chase dreaded cancer away

I have no other suggestions to offer
Except to live life fully each day
Life is such a precious gift
It shouldn't be lived any other way

So love, be loved, love fully
Do good deeds, laugh, make friends
I'm reminded why life's so precious
It's not knowing when it may end

I Wake, Do Nothing, Sleep

I wake, do nothing, sleep
No appointments to keep
No friends left, I sigh
To me who'll say goodbye

Breathing is now so hard
Bedsides with a guard
Just lying here all day
What a price to pay

Memories, almost gone too
Lost, except so few
Body and mind both lost
Age's bitter, bitter cost

Strangers by my bed
She says that we are wed
Did I love, have kids, success
Or was my life a mess?

Helpless, lying here afraid
Tell me my dues are paid
I must escape this agony
Death, please set me free

I should have done the deed
Now I can only plead
Don't they hear my voice?
Please, let me make the choice

No matter what my past
No one deserves this last
There should be a way
For me to choose my last day

Another day, please no
G-d, please let me go
All I can do now is pray
That I won't last the day

Bad Luck?

Sat at a poker table all day
Couldn't win a single hand I played
Of course, I don't expect to always win
Win and lose, the way it's always been

Games of chance I play, come and go
And they have yet to net me much dough
I sometimes think I have terrible luck
Then I remember times I luckily ducked

So many times I have stepped in the street
And nearly been knocked off my feet
So many times I've had narrow escapes
Maybe a watchful angel is guarding my fate

Am I the one in a million struck by lightning?
No. Surely that would be frightening
Has a big tree branch fallen on my head?
Well, no, if it did I'd most likely be dead

Sure, our family has its share of troubles
But don't some others have it double
And isn't having a caring, loving family
The best luck that's been gifted to me

My family is the center of my life
And it all starts with my wonderful wife
And my kids and grandkids too
They make me proud by the good they do

So what if a poker hand doesn't make
And something unexpectedly breaks
If one of the kids brings us bad news
Or something pricy we happen to loose

Yes, such bad luck can make us sad
But the "luck" we make is what makes us glad
Healthy living, hard work, accomplishments
These things, not luck or mere entitlements

So be thankful for the luck you make
Concern for and interest in people you take
For the family you have helped to grow
And the friends you have come to know

And for the good luck you didn't make
To live in a land this great
To be free and to be free to pursue
Whatever dreams are dear to you

So I guess this lesson myself I taught
I'm far, far luckier than I thought
And maybe this lesson has helped you
Appreciate the "luck" that you have too

Decisions

I drove behind a dump truck the other day
For about a mile I couldn't get out of its way
Two arrows painted on the back of that truck
I kept staring at them while I was stuck

One pointing left said "safe side"
The other pointing right said "suicide"
It made me think of the decisions we make
Why some prove helpful; others a mistake

For some there is no luxury to ponder all day
They must be made without any delay
Some we deliberate over so very, very long
To "make sure" we don't get them "wrong"

Personally, I've always been quick to decide
More than once alternatives I should have tried
But decisions that give me the most heartache
Are the ones my loved ones struggle to make

When there are loved ones in your life
You suffer too when they struggle with strife
How involved in their decisions should you be?
Should you jump right in or just wait and see?

Maybe it's best to wait until or if you're asked
But it's hard to sit by and hope you get tasked
Time after time I have struggled with this
The urge to jump right in can be hard to resist

I consider the issue and the loved one involved
And my "success" helping get problems resolved
I'll continue to struggle with what course is best
And maybe what's best is a case-by-case test

It's a dilemma I fear I may never resolve
No matter how well my track record evolves
I'll continue to advise if I think helping is best
Even risking being labeled a meddling pest

The Room

I sat in a room all day
Just where I'll wait to say
With people I've never met
Who knew each other not I bet

No choice had I been given
My absence would not be forgiven
As polite as my "hosts" seemed to be
No chance that I would be set free

I was to be there all day
Circumstances could prolong my stay
But like others I had places to be
So I hoped they'd overlook me

And as I scanned the scene
It was surely not difficult to glean
We were all of a similar mind
Overlooking me would just be fine

Some stretched out on chairs
Some talked quietly in pairs
Some unwrapped and ate food
But mostly folks just seemed to brood

For you see we were given no task
Be still was all that was asked
If/when you're needed we'll call
And oh, the bathroom's down the hall

So we followed their directive to just wait
But wished they'd just open the gate
Did my grandfather view it the same?
Two hundred years ago did they think it lame?

Truth told, my attitude's all wrong
It's a blessing that I belong
I shouldn't begrudge this task
It's a privilege in the US we're asked

By now perhaps you've guessed the place
My attitude truly a disgrace
But I promise to mend my ways
If my stay remains just the one day

So if by chance you still haven't guessed
This was never meant to be a test
The place where I was compelled to be
Was my once every third year jury duty

A Hundred Billion Stars in the Galaxy

The universe is mysterious and so very, very vast
Is it hubris to believe understanding it is a doable task?

A hundred billion stars in our galaxy and a hundred billion galaxies
Might our efforts be better served addressing more earthly queries?

Considerable time, energy, and money is spent exploring the universe
But sadly we continue neglecting to take care of our precious earth

Global warming is just another liberal myth
A hoax to persuade conservatives to become liberals, to switch

It's G-d's will we pass laws to assure every new life gets born
But it's OK to treat social programs that support them with scorn

Supposedly we reach the Divine through our religion
But isn't religion responsible for much of the world's division?

Politics have always been and continue to be conducted fair
And politicians tell us foremost they hold their constituents dear

Equal rights is what the Constitution proclaims
For more than two hundred years we've more than met that aim

Guns don't kill people, people do
The NRA has successfully spent billions to convince us it's true

You can have a mouthful of new permanent teeth in a day
And never again will a care in the world come your way

No matter which of the many, many diet plans you try
Guaranteed, you'll look fabulous and be fully satisfied

Bowflex, Peloton, pick any exercise machine on the market
Guaranteed ten inches, fifty pounds, or whatever your target

So many fallacies, some small and some quite big
Each one intended for some important truth to be rigged

Sadly, we are not vigilant, concerned, or alarmed enough
Because far too often we'll accept such ridiculous stuff

Yes, the universe is vast and largely beyond our comprehension
All the more reason to give things right before us serious attention

A Sad Reality

Friend, oh dear friend, please come and stay with me
The lights are dimming; soon the Lord my host will be

My life has been a simple one, but still I've tried to be
A voice for peace and justice who fought for equality

As my life is now ending some sad truths I can see
People never changing; nations blind to history

Throughout the ages continued disharmony
One people fighting another; each hating foolishly

Oh Lord, please come and take me; I'll go peacefully
If I live another hundred years, no difference would I see

The Hill

Took a walk on a rough path
When I came upon a hill
A little rise upon the ground
Before me it lay so still

Here one can sit, contemplate
The meaning of one's life
To evaluate the sum of it
The good parts and the strife

The trail behind still young and fresh
Beyond the hill lies the new
What accomplishments will I make?
What should I devote my life to?

I pray to G-d I find my path
A dream to follow through
Someday I'll have walked too far
No new path in my view

Before me a wall will rise
Against it I will stand
And though I try to push and push
The future will be banned

And knowing I'm near my end
I'll sit for my final test
Had I done enough in all my years
To earn a peaceful rest?

Here We All Lie, We Died

Here we all lie, we died
Not similar, yet now together
Stricken down by time and the weight of life too
Many remembered but also a forgotten few
Here we all lie, we died

Not bad, nor good
Not cowardice, nor courageous
Not showy, nor humble
But human beings, some surely stumbled
Here we all lie we died

Praise, blame, even accuse, if you must
The path a life takes is surely complex
No one man, nor group, nor any one thing
Can be blamed or credited for what life may bring
Here we all lie, we died

Man's nature has many shades
Good and bad are but two
Without one we could not know the other
Each person alone, yet connected to all others
Soon here all will lie; they will have died

And when your time is done
Will earthly and spiritual judges that surely be
Condemn or praise you for your life's deeds?
Will you rest in peace having planted good seeds?
Think, for here you will lie, you will have died

Just Another Life

Reading this you'll know my time has passed.
I've reached my life's end at last
And mine like most, was "Just Another Life"

What is a "good" person in G-d's scheme
Most of us fall short, someplace in between
Doing both good and bad during our life

Do words like "husband" and father"
Or beloved "wife" and "mother"
On a marker tell the story of a life?

Is this why we strive, why we bother
In the end for some words on a marker
Surely there is more to remembering a life?

We strive to give our life meaning
That effort is what is truly redeeming
And that alone for me does suffice

Strive to always lend a helping hand
When necessary to take a stand
Hopefully, be remembered as someone nice

So if you should visit my stone
There you'll see the message of this poem
And the words—"Just Another Life"

And if I've done this right
Every marker in your sight
May compel you to ponder your life

Sin, Prayer, G-D's Mercy

I sit here among other worshippers, yet alone
Reflecting on all for which I need to atone
My spouse and children sit by my side
As we each look above in G-d to confide

I try, oh how I try, to be earnest in my prayer
Wondering if my words reach G-d's ear
Whether they do or whether they don't
Reflecting and praying is its own anecdote

We say the prayers and we all join in song
And I, too, do my best to sing loudly along
The service helps to raise my spirits high
Being there helps make me want to try

I've been imperfect in so many ways
Sin after sin I commit day after day
From small things like littering on the ground
To big ones I'm not comfortable writing down

Sitting here I vow to be better next year
But as I honestly reflect this is what I fear
I know I've made this same vow in years past
Will anything make this year's pledge last?

The answer I believe lies with G-d not with me
I'm putting my trust in G-d's forgiveness and mercy
What I must do is pray and try to do my best
And seek G-d's mercy when I fall short of G-d's test

Fall at the Beach

Fall at the beach is the very best time
Quiet and peaceful, pristine, free of grime
A blanket, a book, and a stroll on the sand
She and I walking together hand in hand

A bit tired but invigorated from our walk
Quiet time for reflection and a heart-to-heart talk
Getting a bit chilly as the day slowly slips by
We cuddle even closer as we sit side by side

Is it the season that makes the shore best
Or the soft sand, such a good place to rest
Or the sound of the waves crashing to the shore
So calming they beckon to linger some more?

No, like everything else in my life
It's being here together with my wife
So thankful she's here sharing it with me
Luckier, more blessed, no man could ever be

www.ingramcontent.com/pod-product-compliance
Lightning Source LLC
Chambersburg PA
CBHW050805160726
48004CB00002B/716